The Tiger
Who Came
to Tea

The Tiger
Who
Came
to Tea

written and illustrated by
Judith Kerr

HarperCollins *Children's Books*

For Tacy and Matty

Other books by Judith Kerr include:

Mog the Forgetful Cat

Mog's Christmas

Mog and the Baby

Mog in the Dark

Mog's Amazing Birthday Caper

Mog and Bunny

Mog and Barnaby

Mog on Fox Night

Mog and the Granny

Mog and the V.E.T.

Mog's Bad Thing

Goodbye Mog

Birdie Halleluyah!

The Other Goose

Goose in a hole

Twinkles, Arthur and Puss

First published in hardback in Great Britain by William Collins Sons & Co Ltd in 1968. First published in paperback by Picture Lions in 1973. New edition published in hardback by HarperCollins Children's Books in 2006. This edition published in hardback in 2008

10 9 8 7 6 5 4 3 2 1
ISBN-13: 978-0-00-782659-9
ISBN-10: 0-00-782659-1

Visit our website at: www.harpercollinschildrensbooks.co.uk

Printed and bound in China

Once there was a little girl called Sophie,
and she was having tea with her mummy
in the kitchen.
Suddenly there was a ring at the door.

Sophie's mummy said,
"I wonder who that can be.

THIS WEEK'S SPECIAL
FARMHOUSE CHICKENS

UNITED
DAIRIES

It can't be the milkman
because he came this morning.

And it can't be the boy from the grocer because this isn't the day he comes.

And it can't be Daddy because he's got his key.

We'd better open the door and see."

Sophie opened
the door, and
there was a big,
furry, stripy tiger.
The tiger said,
"Excuse me, but
I'm very hungry.
Do you think
I could have
tea with you?"
Sophie's mummy
said, "Of course,
come in."

So the tiger came into the kitchen and sat down at the table.

Sophie's mummy said, "Would you like a sandwich?"
But the tiger didn't just take one sandwich.
He took all the sandwiches on the plate
and swallowed them in one big mouthful.
Owp!

And he still looked hungry,
so Sophie passed him the buns.

But again the tiger didn't eat just one bun.
He ate all the buns on the dish.
And then he ate all the biscuits
and all the cake,
until there was nothing
left to eat on the table.

So Sophie's mummy said,
"Would you like a drink?"
And the tiger drank
all the milk in the milk jug
and all the tea in the teapot.

And then he looked round the kitchen

to see what else he could find.

He ate all the supper
that was cooking in the saucepans…

…and all the food in the fridge,

…and all the packets and tins in the cupboard…

…and he drank all the milk,
and all the orange juice,
and all Daddy's beer,
and all the water in the tap.

Then he said,
"Thank you for my
nice tea. I think I'd
better go now."

And he went.

Sophie's mummy said, "I don't know what to do.
I've got nothing for Daddy's supper, the tiger has
eaten it all."

And Sophie found she couldn't have her bath
because the tiger had drunk all the water in the tap.

Just then Sophie's daddy came home.

So Sophie and her mummy told him what had
happened, and how the tiger had eaten all the food
and drunk all the drink.

And Sophie's daddy said, "I know what we'll do.
I've got a very good idea. We'll put on our coats
and go to a café."

So they went out in the dark, and all the street lamps were lit, and all the cars had their lights on, and they walked down the road to a café.

And they had a lovely supper with sausages and chips and ice cream.

In the morning
Sophie and her mummy
went shopping
and they bought
lots more things to eat.

And they also bought
a very big tin of
Tiger Food, in case
the tiger should
come to tea again.

But he never did.